THE KING of KEJI

Written by Jan L. Coates

Illustrated by Patsy MacKinnon

NIMBUS
PUBLISHING LTD

Nimbus Publishing Limited
3731 Mackintosh St, Halifax, NS B3K 5A5
(902) 455-4286 nimbus.ca

Printed and bound in China

NB1091

Design: Heather Bryan

Library and Archives Canada Cataloguing in Publication

      Coates, Jan, 1960-, author
      The king of Keji / written by Jan L. Coates ; illustrated by Patsy MacKinnon.
      ISBN 978-1-77108-281-5 (pbk.)

1. Kejimkujik National Park and National Historic Site (N.S.)—Juvenile fiction. I. MacKinnon, Patsy,
1952-, illustrator II. Title.

PS8605.O238K56 2015   jC813'.6   C2014-907784-X

Nimbus Publishing acknowledges the financial support for its publishing activities from the
Government of Canada through the Canada Book Fund (CBF) and the Canada Council for the Arts,
and from the Province of Nova Scotia through Film & Creative Industries Nova Scotia. We are pleased
to work in partnership with Film & Creative Industries Nova Scotia to develop and promote our
creative industries for the benefit of all Nova Scotians.

For my treasures, Liam and Shannon.—J. L. C.

For Dean and his grandpas.—P. M.

"Ben's always king of the castle," Jacob said. "I'm tired of being the dirty rascal."

Gramps grinned. "I ever tell you about the time I was a king?"

Jacob frowned. "King of the castle?"

Gramps shook his head. "King of Keji. Kejimkujik National Park and National Historic Site. A real treasure trove, and one of my favorite places."

"I want to be a king. Can we go?" Jacob asked. "This weekend?"

"Maybe. But it's a big job, learning to be a king."

Saturday morning, they left right after breakfast. They put up the tent first thing, then Gramps and Jacob set off on a hike.

"Don't forget your camera," Gramps said. "The King of Keji needs superior treasure-hunting skills."

"What about a shovel?" Jacob asked.

"It's not buried treasure. It's hidden treasure," Gramps said.

"Like a scavenger hunt?" Jacob asked.

Gramps nodded. "For things that are valuable and rare. Now, what would a king use to go hiking?"

"That big stick thingy."

"A sceptre."

Jacob picked up a piece of driftwood. "How about this?"

"I like it!" Gramps said.

"No jewels, but it's just my size. Take my picture?" Jacob asked.

Click.

"What other treasures do kings have?" Gramps said. "Amber, sapphires, antiques …"

"Diamonds, turquoise, crystal, rubies…" Jacob rubbed his hands together. "And money."

"Pearls, jade, emeralds, ebony and ivory," Gramps added.

"Are all those things here?" Jacob frowned.

Gramps nodded. "We can't take most of them home, though. Except for pictures."

"Whoa! Look at that giant tree grabbing onto that rock!" Jacob looked up, way up.

"A hemlock—it's been around even longer than me." Gramps chuckled. "About three hundred years or so. See any valuables there?"

"Hmmm…the leaves are green. Emerald green!" Jacob tried to wrap his arms around the enormous trunk. "And the stone's got shiny bits of silver in it."

Click.

"Shhh!" Gramps pointed into the woods.

Jacob stopped walking. He almost stopped breathing.

The doe and her fawn looked up as a chatty chipmunk scampered up a hemlock.

Click.

"Amber," Jacob whispered. "Their eyes."

They joined a guided hike with a Mi'kmaw interpreter and meandered along the lakeshore. "Why do we have to take off our shoes?" Jacob asked.

"These petroglyphs have been here for centuries," Gramps said, pointing to the stone engravings. "They're an important part of the history of the Mi'kmaw people and must be protected."

Click.

"Let's sit on this log and have our lunch," Gramps said. "Keep your eyes open."

"Mmmm…" Jacob put one hand above his eyes and squinted at the lake. "Diamonds!" he shouted. "Sun diamonds sparkling on the water!"

Click.

"Can we go for a canoe ride?" Jacob asked after supper. "Please, Gramps?"

They paddled out into the middle of the glassy lake.

"The trees all have twins," Jacob said.

"Don't see a perfect reflection like that every day," Gramps said.

Click.

A family of loons glided along next to the bank.

"Ebony," Gramps said. "And ivory. Like piano keys."

"Except for the fuzzy babies," Jacob whispered.

Click.

They built a fire, then made s'mores, chocolate marshmallow ooze.

"Pearls!" Jacob held up his drippy marshmallow.

Click.

"I must almost be the King of Keji." Jacob licked his fingers.

"Because of all the treasure we've found?"

"Well, that." Jacob slapped his arms. "And my billion bloodthirsty enemies!"

They curled up together under a velvety blanket of stars.

"More diamonds." Jacob yawned up at the sky. "Only I'm too sleepy for pictures."

The lonely cry of the loon and the song of the lake gently lulled them to sleep.

"How's your treasure hunt going so far?" Gramps asked in the morning.

Jacob counted on his fingers. "My sceptre, emeralds, silver, amber, twin trees, antiques, diamonds, ebony and ivory, and pearls. Is ten enough?"

Grampy shook his head. "Not quite. We'll drive over to Keji Seaside today. See what treasure's in store for us there."

They hiked along the wooded path at Keji Seaside. On the boardwalk, Jacob stopped and crouched down beside a small pool. Two frogs splashed up onto a mossy stone. "Jade," Jacob said.

Click.

The boardwalk across the open salt marsh led them to the ocean. "Turquoise!" Jacob ran down the hill to the beach. "Lots and lots of turquoise!"

Click.

Jacob wiggled his toes in the warm sand. "What do those signs say, over by that fence?"

"Beach closed. Piping plovers nesting," Gramps read. "They're an endangered species, and this is one of the few places they nest."

Jacob put the binoculars up to his eyes. "Awesome!"

Gramps nodded. "And all too rare."

Click.

"Look at the size of this shell." Jacob bent down and picked it up. "What is it?"

Gramps smiled. "It's a moon snail. Pretty, isn't it?"

"A giant pearl. Only I'm glad the giant snail's not home," Jacob said. "And money! A sand dollar."

Click.

Gramps peered through the binoculars.

"What do you see?" Jacob asked. "And what's that spooky moaning sound?"

"Take a look for yourself," Gramps said.

"Awesome! Seals. Six all crammed onto that one big rock."

"Any treasure there?" Gramps asked.

"They're so cool. They *are* treasure. Better than jewels."

Jacob climbed up on the boulders to get a better look.

Click.

They drove back to the campground, arriving at the tent just as Jacob's belly started grumbling.

"Let's eat down by the lake. See if we can catch the sunset," Gramps said.

As the sun sank into the trees, fingers of gold, orange, and red sparkled across the lake.

"Whoa!" Jacob said. "Rubies and gold!"

Click.

A squirrel scolded them awake in the morning. "So, am I the King of Keji yet?" Jacob asked.

Gramps smiled. "Almost. But a king needs a crown. Did you see anything you could use to make yourself a crown?"

Jacob crawled out of the tent and looked around the campsite. "Maybe."

"You go ahead while I pack up," Gramps said.

Jacob found a piece of twine in the campsite next door. He cut it into three pieces, braided them together, then tied it to fit his head. He gathered some fallen oak leaves, red berries, and green and yellow grasses and worked them into the braid. A small crystal stuck in the center with pine sap made it perfect.

Jacob sat down on a giant boulder and leaned back against a tree. "Ta-da! Like my throne?"

Gramps put one hand on Jacob's head. "I now pronounce you the King of Keji!"

Click.

"And best of all," Gramps said, "you've left all the treasure we found for others to enjoy."

Jacob nodded and stood up. "Now that I'm a king, does that mean I get to tell you what to do?"

Gramps bowed. "At your service, Your Royal Highness. Your every wish is my command."

"Could we stop for ice cream, then?" Jacob asked, leaning his sceptre up against his throne and setting his crown down beside it. "Please?"

"One s'mores ice cream cone coming up—for the King of Keji!"

"And one for my faithful servant," Jacob said. "Onward, Sir Gramps. I can't wait to show Ben all my treasure!"

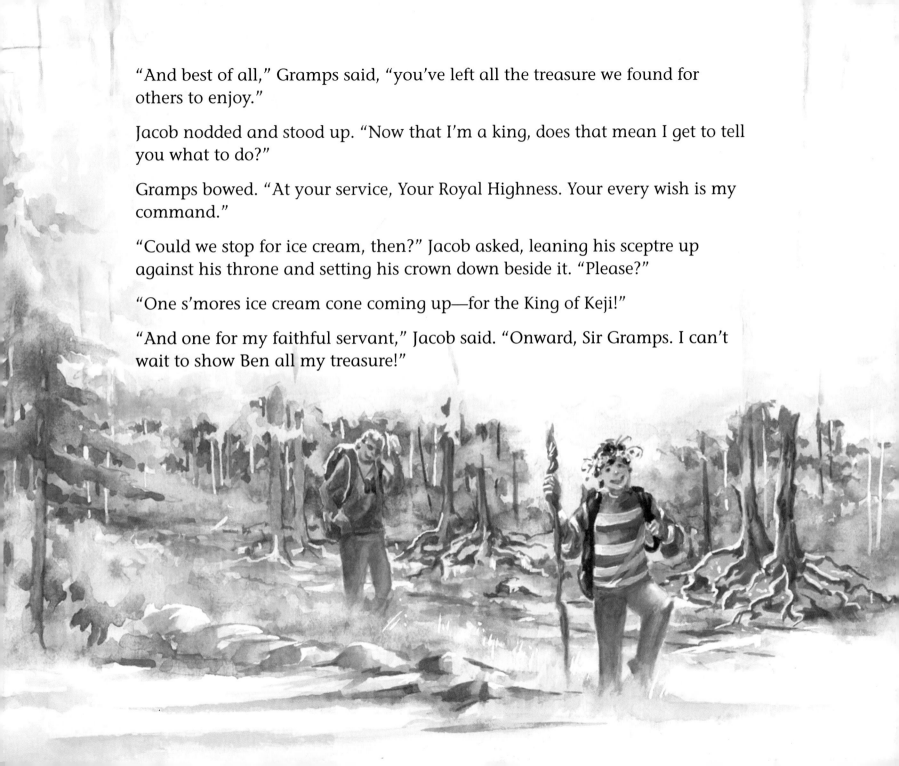

Kejimkujik National Park and National Historic Site, commonly known as "Keji," is a magnificent and treasured piece of Nova Scotia. Canoeing its pristine waterways, hiking or biking its woodland trails, swimming, camping, and exploring the wildlife and plants—the possibilities for pleasure are endless. From strolling the white sandy beaches of Kejimkujik Seaside while seals bask in the turquoise waters, to stargazing, to guided walks among the ancient hemlock trees and Mi'kmaw petroglyphs, Keji is a wonderful place for families to learn and play together while surrounded by nature at its best.

JAN L. COATES